The
Kwanzaa
Contest

Miriam Moore and Penny Taylor

Illustrated by Laurie Spencer

Hyperion Books for Children
New York

To the world's best mother and friend, Dutt Moore
–M. M.

To my most demanding critics, my wonderful
daughters, Natalie and Nacole, and their cousins,
Justina and Louis
–P. T.

Text © 1996 by Miriam Moore and Penny Taylor.
Illustrations © 1996 by Laurie Spencer.

Printed in the United States of America.

3 5 7 9 10 8 6 4 2

This book is set in 16-point Berkeley Book.

Library of Congress Cataloging-in-Publication Data
Moore, Miriam.
The Kwanzaa contest / Miriam Moore and Penny Taylor.
p.   cm.
Summary: Even though he lacks the confidence of his older sister
Latrice, third grader Ron makes himself enter the Kwanzaa
contest in which he reveals the talent of his hands.
ISBN 0-7868-2336-4 (lib. bdg.)—ISBN 0-7868-1122-6 (pbk.)
[1. Kwanzaa—Fiction. 2. Afro-Americans—Fiction. 3. Brothers
and sisters—Fiction. 4. Contests—Fiction. 5. Handicraft—
Fiction.] I. Taylor, Penny. II. Title.
PZ7.M7874Kw   1996
[Fic]—dc2   95-26631

Contents

1
Miss Know-It-All

"Ron, where are you? I need you. *Now!*"

Ronald cringed. It was his older sister, Latrice. "Here," he answered.

"Where's here?"

"Here's here." He rattled a pot by Gran's stove.

"Cute," called Latrice. "I just hope you are not messin' with that loose cabinet knob."

"So what if I am? Gran said I could try some glue on it." He touched the loose knob gently.

"Because you'll break it off, that's why. Remember what you did to Gran's pot handle?"

Ronald looked at the knob now lying in his

1

hand. How did she know that would happen? For the zillionth time he wondered why his sister was always such a know-it-all.

Latrice was in the sixth grade and he was in the third. And she *always* thought she was smarter than Ronald. That really steamed him.

And the worst part was, Ronald sometimes thought so, too. After all, Latrice could read a whole book in one afternoon. Then she would talk about it all through supper. Gran loved to hear about Latrice's books.

But not Ron. Who wanted to ruin Gran's great dinners with school stuff?

Latrice could also dance and sing. She loved to give concerts in the front room. Gran and Ron were her "invited guests."

But Ron usually "invited" himself to the bathroom. One scarf around Latrice's neck and he knew a sudden bathroom call was coming. She loved to dance with scarves.

"But you're smart, too, baby," Gran would often say to Ronald. "Everybody is smart in different ways. Gran's Little Man is smart in his hands. See?"—and his grandmama would usually point to the gold flower box—"Why, it's the prettiest flower box in the whole project."

"Oh, Gran, it's just cardboard," Ronald would say. "Anybody can glue cardboard and paint flowers."

"And this box you made for my thread," Gran would say. "It's the prettiest box on God's green earth." This always brought a hug. "Yessir, my Ronald's got mighty smart hands."

But many days Ronald would just stare at his hands. They held only comic books, not important books. In fact, they spent most of their time changing TV channels.

"So what's so smart about my hands?" Ronald had asked out loud one day.

"Nothing," Latrice had answered. "Your hands

are not smart." She had glanced at his hands. "They are not even clean. Go wash."

"Ronald!"

Ronald jumped up. He had completely forgotten Latrice. She now sounded spittin' mad. "Hold on. I'm coming." He dropped the broken knob into his shirt pocket. In the front room, he found her shoving the sofa. She held a piece of paper.

"What's that?"

"A sofa that's too heavy, that's what. Give me a hand. I need to practice some steps."

"No, I mean that paper."

"The rules of the Kwanzaa Contest," she announced. She suddenly stood straight, then twirled around the room.

"What Kwanzaa Contest?"

"The one down at the community center." She tilted gracefully. "It's to celebrate Kwanzaa. That's a festival for African Americans." She

then took a deep bow. "It takes place the week after Christmas, but this year the contest's late. The community center had to be closed for remodeling."

"I don't get it." Ronald flopped down onto the sofa.

"That's right. You don't." Latrice flashed a challenging smile. " 'Cause I will. All fifty dollars."

Ronald bolted upright.

"They will give fifty dollars to the best African display," she explained.

"Fifty dollars?" repeated Ronald. He adjusted his baseball cap. "That's a lot of money."

Latrice stretched forward. "Not when you can dance the dance of a Zulu queen." She twirled again. "I will dance a dance of our people."

"Me, too!" said Ronald.

Latrice laughed. "You? Dance?"

"No, but I'll do something."

"What?" asked Latrice. "Stumble over your own feet? Bump your head? That is what you do best, Bro."

Ronald did not answer. He yanked his baseball cap down tighter. Why, I bet Big Bad Butler's never even seen that much money, he thought. Orlando Butler was his real name, but all the kids at school called him Big Bad Butler 'cause he was so big and so mean. Punching out kids was his favorite sport.

"And Ron?" called Latrice from the door.

"What?"

"You better glue that knob back fast. Gran will be home any minute."

"What knob?" Ronald tried to sound cool.

"The one you're hiding in your shirt pocket," answered Latrice smugly as she danced out the door.

2
The Secret Pact

That night Ronald could not sleep. He heard the warehouse trains. He heard Mrs. Perkins overhead yelling at old Mr. Perkins.

Ronald also heard the usual sirens. They made him feel glad he was in his own bed, with Gran and Latrice just a thin wall away.

Then there was Scat-Rat, his noisy guinea pig. Scat-Rat used to belong to Latrice. She won it for a science project. But one day Big Bad Butler was sent to the board. When he passed Ron's desk, he slipped on Ron's New York Yankees pencil. He went sprawling down the aisle.

No one dared to laugh.

"I'm gonna get you good," Butler hissed as he picked himself up.

"For what?" Ron asked.

"For this!" And Big Bad Butler crushed the pencil, dropping the splinters on Ron's head. Ron didn't even miss his pencil.

Ron cringed. Oh, man, he thought. I better make a run for home after school.

But that afternoon he wasn't fast enough. As he rounded the corner at the Pay-for-Less store, Big Bad Butler stepped out of the doorway. "Why are you in such a hurry?"

Ron stopped and didn't even answer. He just squeezed his eyes shut and waited for the worst.

Pow! The next thing Ron knew, he was on the ground, holding his bleeding nose. "A punched nose ain't nothing to what's waiting for you." Big Bad Butler turned around. "Mess with me again and you'll see."

That afternoon Latrice helped clean him up,

then went to her room. She brought out Jamal, her guinea pig. He was living in a shoe box. She gave him to Ron.

"Call him Scat-Rat," she insisted. "That way you'll say 'Scat-Rat' so often it'll come natural to say to that bully Butler."

Ron didn't say anything. Latrice wasn't afraid of anyone, not even Big Bad Butler. But then again *she* never had Butler stand so close that his chin could rest on her head. Ron could still feel Butler's hot breath on his forehead.

Latrice had never had Big Bad Butler punch her in the nose, either.

"You can still keep him in your room some," Ron offered. He couldn't believe Jamal was now his. "I'll make him a brand-new cage and every-thing."

"Forget it," Latrice said. "He's yours. Smell and all. Besides, he scratches all night long."

Soon Ron turned his dresser top into a

Scat-Rat circus. He made exercise wheels out of big jar lids. He formed a trampoline out of a rubber glove. He even painted clowns and a tent show around Scat-Rat's new, bigger box. Gran was so proud, she showed it to some neighbors.

Scat-Rat was the nicest thing Latrice had ever given Ron. Latrice even began to walk home with him every afternoon. But that was because Gran told her to.

But what Ron heard in his head was louder than the train, Mrs. Perkins, or Scat-Rat's scratching. The words "fifty dollars" chugged with the rhythm of the engine. Fifty dollars. Fifty dollars. Fifty dollars.

Fifty dollars would buy Gran thread of every color. It would even buy him that hammer and screwdriver he had wanted for Christmas. With those tools he could fix every knob and handle in the whole project.

"Right, Scat-Rat?" he whispered in the dark.

Scat-Rat just kept on scratching.

Ron rolled over and socked his pillow. But what could he do? No one would pay fifty dollars to watch him change TV channels.

He sat up against the headboard. This way he could wear his magic baseball cap, brim backward. It had never failed him with good ideas.

Mr. Sanu! Yes!

Mr. Sanu was from Africa. He had come one day to Ronald's class. He had brought pretty wooden carvings of animals and people. Ron had wanted to learn how to carve like that. Mr. Sanu had said they were from his native country, Nigeria. He had told stories about each one. Then he had shown Ron some carving techniques.

"Yes!" whispered Ron to himself in the dark. He slapped his cap on the pillow. "And I can carve. I will make an African carving. After all, I am African American."

The next morning Ron sat staring into his yucky bowl of oatmeal. He tried to talk to Gran alone. But Latrice was busy describing her Kwanzaa costume. So he waited and waited.

But Latrice kept on talking. "So when I get home we'll cut out a pattern, okay?" she said to Gran.

"I'll do my best," Gran said as she kissed Latrice. "But I may be running late."

"No problem." Latrice waved as she twirled out of the room.

Oh yes, big problem, thought Ronald as he stared at his bowl of disgusting raisin oatmeal. Yuck! Raisins always reminded him of dried-up roaches.

But after churning his cereal, he convinced Gran he had eaten enough. He then told her of his plan to enter the Kwanzaa Contest.

"A carving, you say?"

"Yes. An African carving like Mr. Sanu's. He spoke to our class once—he's from Africa." Ronald looked down at his hands. "But it probably won't look like anything. Just a dumb hunk of nothing."

Gran shook her hands free of dishwater. She came over and took Ronald's hands in hers, squeezing them. "Oh, but you know better. These hands are rich—I say—rich with talent."

Ronald did not know about that. He just knew he wanted to be rich with fifty dollars. "So I can have your carving knife? The one you use to cut up chicken?"

"Oh, Gran's got a better knife than that." She then handed him a table knife.

"But this is not sharp." He ran his thumb over the edge. "It couldn't carve a . . . a lump of oatmeal."

His grandmother handed him two large cakes of green soap. "But it will carve these."

She smiled broadly. "Then you won't cut those smart hands."

Ronald frowned. Who could win anything with a dull knife and dumb bars of soap? But as he stared at the soap, one of Mr. Sanu's stories came to mind.

"I'm going out on the fire escape, Gran."

"You be careful, you hear?"

He gathered his knife and soap and headed for the window. "And, Gran?" He was already halfway through the window.

"What's that, baby?"

"Promise, promise, promise you won't tell Latrice anything about my plan."

"Oh, she's too busy with her own plans to win."

Ronald jerked the brim of his cap down tight. That's just what he was afraid of.

3
The Monster on the Fire Escape

Ronald loved his seat in class. He was two seats up from Big Bad Butler. That meant he was too far away to be rammed by Butler's knees or jabbed by Butler's ruler . . . or worse.

And Tanya Harwell sat between them. Tanya had a voice like a fire alarm. If Butler ever messed with Tanya, her squeal would easily bring the police, three blocks away. So Ron felt safe and out of reach.

Unless Tanya was sick. Then Big Bad Butler loved to flick spitwads at the back of Ron's head. Hour after hour he was pelted. And every time one would land under Ron's collar, Butler would whisper "Score!" One day the spitwad score actually climbed to nineteen by lunch.

So every morning Ron waited to see Mrs. Harwell's blue Toyota pull up by the school's flagpole. One sight of Tanya's beaded braids and he knew his day was looking up.

Today, as usual, Tanya was present. But after roll call, the teacher sent her on an errand.

Ron's heart thudded.

By the time Tanya was back, though, Big Bad Butler had collared only his sixth spitwad down Ron's shirt. The morning wasn't all that terrible, Ron decided as he finally ran out to recess.

But out by the tetherball court, Butler began to chant *"Gran's Little Man . . . Gran's Little Man . . . "*

Some of the other boys now chimed in. Big Bad Butler then made kissy sounds on the back of his hand.

Everyone laughed.

Ron went over and stood by the big tree. He began to study the trunk, but really he had to get his eyes to cool it. They were starting to sting, so he opened them real wide, faking a yawn.

I wish I'd never made that stupid key ring, he thought for the zillionth time as he stripped a piece of bark. Who would have known the summer-camp counselor would display everyone's leather craft? And right out in the middle of the community center, too!

Every kid in the projects had read his surprise for Gran. *I Love You*, signed *Gran's Little Man* on a big oval leather ring.

That was just between Gran and me, Ron had wanted to shout that day at that counselor.

But not anymore. Not with Big Bad Butler. He started calling Ron that the first week of school. He started in the cafeteria line. Then he called him Gran's Little Man whenever Ron was sent to the board. He even said it over the loud-speaker one day. He had blurted it out just before he read the day's menu.

Everyone in the class had laughed but Ron. He had just put his head on the desk and made a book roof over it.

Finally the recess bell rang and Ron could stop stripping the bark off the tree. The rest of the day was uneventful, and he made it home without running into Butler.

Ron was glad to be home—at last. He closed his door, threw his books on the bed, and went over to Scat-Rat's circus cage. "You're lucky, you know that?"

The guinea pig came up and sniffed at Ron's finger.

"You don't have to go to school. All you have to do is be a guinea pig."

Pig. The thought made him grab his practice soap and knife.

He held up the chunk of soap and studied it. Mr. Sanu had told a story about the sacred image of the alligator. Would his carving ever look like an alligator?

He slipped out on the fire escape and began to trim the sides. No alligator is fat, he told himself as he adjusted his baseball cap.

After a while Gran peered through the window. "Hey, I like your turtle."

Ron frowned. He then continued to trim the sides of his alligator.

He then went bump, bump, bump with his knife. He held it up again. Good, he thought. Now he is starting to have a rough-and-tough skin.

Bump, bump, bump went the knife again. Just as he was about to start on the long tail, Gran peered through the window again. "Oh, what a wonderful elephant!"

Ron didn't have time to frown. Latrice was

now coming through the door. He quickly turned his back and slumped down under the window.

"This is no elephant," he grumbled. Then he noticed its long round nose. At least it won't look like an elephant for long, he hoped. Quickly he began to shave, shave, shave the long fat nose.

Now it was not fat but alligator-flat. That's better, he thought as he looked at his turtle-elephant-alligator. At last the alligator part was starting to win.

But he could hear his sister dancing inside. She kept telling Gran, "Watch this!" and, "What about this?" Then it grew silent.

"Knock, knock."

Ronald crouched down. "Go away, Trice."

"What're you doing out there?"

"Something."

"Cute. I know! You've done something bad,

so Gran locked you out." She laughed. "Right, Gran?"

"Just leave the little man alone. He's busy making something."

Ronald held his breath.

"Making what?"

"Never you mind, baby girl. Here, let's try this pattern."

"I know," laughed Latrice. "Ronald's busy making mistakes. That's his favorite hobby."

He looked at the green form in his hand. Was this a mistake? If I showed it to Latrice, he wondered, would she see a green alligator about to be born?

He sat there, motionless. He began to shave the nose again. Oh, what does she know about alligators anyway? "Only if they dance," he murmured to himself. The thought of dancing alligators made him smile.

4
Mystery in the Park

Every afternoon after school Ron ran to his room. He grabbed his knife and carving from under the pillow. Then he slipped out onto the fire escape.

On the way, Gran always got her hug and kiss, but she was now very busy. The Kwanzaa Contest was just five days away and Latrice's costume was still too big.

But that didn't stop her from dancing past the window every afternoon. "Watch my steps, Ron. I am Queen of the Zulus. See?" And she would sway and weave to her song. "I just wish I had a headband."

But Ronald did not look. He was too busy carving. Besides, she might just catch a peek at his alligator.

Then, of course, she would just laugh, as usual. "Why, that alligator has no eyes!" she would say. "My brother has carved a blind alligator. What a dum-dum."

Just the thought made Ron flinch.

And the truth was, the eyes were causing big problems. Ron had carved eyes on every bar of soap Gran had. But he still did not like their look. And the worst part was he didn't know what was wrong. He just knew they looked more like bee sting welts than alligator eyes.

"I know!" He grabbed a mirror.

He thought mean thoughts. He thought of Big Bad Butler. He thought of his sister winning the contest.

His eyes narrowed.

"Yes!" he shouted. "That's it!"

Now he shaved the bumpy eyes of the alligator to narrow slits. He held up his carving.

"Yes!" He ran his hand over the bumpy skin and across the narrow eyes. Not bad, he thought as he turned his carving slowly from side to side. It certainly looked better than his first two practice bars. Even Latrice would not call this a turtle or an elephant now, he decided. What's more, it had eyes and everything.

Now all I've got to do is remember every part of Mr. Sanu's alligator story, he thought, and he turned his baseball cap backward. A lot of work still lay ahead.

The next day at school Ron sensed trouble. The morning had gone too well: Big Bad Butler had not called him one name. He didn't even try to tie Ron's shoelaces to his chair. So something was bound to go wrong after lunch. But after lunch Big Bad Butler slept through math and spelling. Still, Ron knew disaster was waiting somewhere. After all, it was still early and seven long blocks to home.

"Where are your books?" Latrice asked as she met him by the flagpole.

"I don't need any. She didn't give us any homework."

"I don't believe that."

Ron rammed his hands into his jacket. "Okay, so don't."

"Mrs. Clements always gave math problems." Latrice gave her backpack a heave upward. "I remember 'cause I always got a plus on my paper."

Ron didn't answer. Mrs. Clements had given math homework, but he'd left it stuffed in his desk. He could finish it before class started. Part of it, anyway. This way he had all afternoon to work on his alligator.

They crossed the street and headed down by the row houses. Latrice stood on tiptoe, straining to see. "Yea! Nobody's sitting out." She broke into a run. "First!"

Ron ran, too. He loved their game. When no one was sitting out on the row house steps, they liked to play a rhyme game. Whoever was first would make up a line while hopping up on the first step. Then the other person had to follow with a line that rhymed with the one before it. By the time they got up to the top step, Ron and Latrice had usually made up a poem.

Latrice hopped up flat-footed. "There once was a polka-dot pig in my hat."

Ron hopped behind her, then paused. "But I just clapped my hands and said, 'Scat!'"

"But my poor hat is now so flat!"

"It looks like a drowned rat," Ron offered.

"So-o-o," Latrice drew out, hesitating. "So, I now wear a dead rat for a hat."

They both laughed so hard at the top step that Ron teetered backward. Latrice caught him.

"My turn." Ron thought for a minute. He wanted a tough one. "Okay, okay, here goes: There once was a contest for Kwanzaa."

"No fair," Latrice protested. "No words rhyme with Kwanzaa."

"Says who?"

"Says me."

"Okay: There once was a prize of fifty dollars."

Latrice hopped down behind him. "For any crybaby who hollers."

Ron hopped down. "But so many were crying, there's no denying—"

Latrice squealed as she landed behind him. "The dancer Latrice wins the fifty dollars!"

She then broke into a run. "Gotcha that time."

"No you didn't." Ron ran as fast as he could. "You didn't follow my line."

But Latrice kept running and laughing. Ron

did, too. Suddenly, by Riverfront Park, Latrice came to an abrupt stop. "Listen," she whispered.

At first Ron couldn't hear anything, but then he began to hear strange thumping sounds. "What's that?"

Latrice held her finger to her lips. She pointed behind a clump of bushes. There were two boys wielding long sticks. One was trying to knock the other's stick from his hand.

Ron swallowed hard. One was Big Bad Butler.

"Hey!" Latrice shouted, running into the park. "Hey, cut that out!"

Again Ron swallowed hard but followed her anyway. Big Bad Butler was bad enough unarmed . . . but with a weapon?

"What do you want?" the bully demanded.

She told him they better stop fighting or she was going to get somebody.

Butler spit out a laugh. "That's how much you know, girl." He caught sight of Ron. "And what're you doing here?"

"Okay, I'm telling." Latrice started to turn.

"We're not fighting," Big Bad Butler added quickly. "We're practicing. Right, Calvin?"

The tall boy with the long face and deep-set eyes nodded. Ron had seen him in the halls.

"Practicing what?" Latrice demanded, folding her arms.

Ron wished with all his might she would just walk away clean. Where did she get so much gumption anyway? A boy like Orlando Butler could blow sky-high any minute.

"For something over at the center," the other boy offered. "There's going to be a competition with big money."

"The Kwanzaa Contest?" squealed Latrice, who then fell into fits of laughter. "You're going to fight in the contest?"

Big Bad Butler came over to her. He held one stick out. "See this? This here is hand-carved. The boys in the Pondo tribe in Africa used hand-carved sticks in their games."

"This was carved in Africa?" Latrice reached out, but he snatched it away.

"No, it's my Paw-Paw's walking cane. He carved it back in Mississippi." He ran his hand over it slowly. "He gave it to Mama before he died. But carving is carving."

Ron wanted a closer look at the beautiful carving. It looked cool with its vines twining everywhere up the dark wood. But he didn't dare say a word.

"And what're you staring at, Little Man?" Big Bad Butler suddenly demanded, glaring at Ron.

"He's with me," Latrice informed him. "Let's go, Ron. We wouldn't want to delay these prizewinners."

Ron was very glad to go. He almost didn't

mind the usual chants behind him . . . *Gran's Little Man . . . Gran's Little Man.*

But once they were back on the sidewalk, Latrice demanded to know how they knew his nickname.

"That's my business." He didn't want to dig up that camp fiasco now. Besides, the two boys were still mocking and chanting.

Suddenly Latrice swung around on her heel. "You leave my brother alone," she shouted, stomping her foot. "You hear?"

This brought a mocking sound of fright from the boys.

"Cut it out, Trice," Ron whispered. "It's okay. Really, it is."

5
The Big Surprise

"Call out my spelling words," Latrice ordered as she dropped the backpack on the table. "Just sound them out and I'll know which one you mean."

Ron groaned. "Can't you wait for Gran? I've got to feed Scat-Rat."

But she already had her notebook open, handing it to him. "I have a test, so let's go."

"But it's Friday—"

"*Ron!*"

He flopped down on the couch. "Okay, okay, but just one time. I mean it."

She didn't answer. She was too busy scanning the list.

"I wonder how he did that?" said Ron.

She looked up. "Who did what?"

"That walking cane. I wonder how Butler's granddaddy made those vines so smooth and twisting."

"Practice, I guess." She handed him the notebook. "Mix them up and ask me all of them."

"Carving any curve is the hardest. I found that out. It has to be rounded, then rounded some more."

Latrice sat down on the floor, lotus-style. "Very interesting. Now hit me with some words. I want to bug this test."

Ron tried to focus on the paper. But he was still thinking of that hand-carved cane. Now *that* was real talent! He just hoped Big Bad Butler would not tell the judge he carved it himself.

"Carved." The word made him think of his alligator waiting in his room. Two nights ago he had thought he had an okay alligator at last—

with mean eyes, a flat tail, the works.

Then a hind leg had broken off!

Ron had just sat there, numb. The contest was Saturday and he was stuck with a *three-legged* alligator!

But after working almost all night on yet another of Gran's green soaps, he had another carving within spittin' distance of the three-legged one. In fact, its head was even better. But it would still take hours to shape into something really cool.

And what was he doing now? Wasting time calling out dumb spelling words so Latrice could make another A+.

When he finally got back to his room, he kept thinking about the smooth rounding of the cane's vines. He picked up his new alligator and began to trim, then smooth, its bent legs. Again and again, he followed the outline of the vines he had seen.

Not bad, he decided as he held it up for the zillionth time. I think Mr. Sanu would be proud of these legs.

"What do you think, Scat-Rat? How's that for alligator legs?"

But Scat-Rat continued to burrow under the newspaper in the bottom of his cage.

Ron was so tired, his chin kept bouncing off his chest. But he still had to work on his speech. "Keep scratchin', Scat-Rat," he said. "You've heard how I always mess up the ending. Keep me awake till I get it right."

The next morning Ronald's eyes flew open. He saw only darkness. What time is it? he wondered, sitting up. Then his baseball cap fell off his face and he could see the bright sun. Man, it's late, he concluded.

Quickly he grabbed his jeans off the floor. This was the big day. He selected his green

T-shirt. "Green is the color of money," he announced to Scat-Rat as he cupped the guinea pig to his chest. "Wish me luck." He thought of Butler's fancy carved stick. "I'm gonna need it, big-time."

"Your oatmeal is ready," Gran called from the kitchen.

"Thanks, but I'm not hungry." Ronald was already standing at the door. His carving was in his hand. And his speech was in his head. He had said it a dozen times to Scat-Rat around midnight. He just hoped the judge would like them both.

"Hurry up, Latrice," he shouted toward the bathroom door.

"Hurry up what?" answered Latrice. "It's only eight-thirty, Bro. The contest doesn't start till ten." She made a sputtering noise. "Gran, tell him."

But Ron was out of there. He ran down the

narrow steps and out on the stoop. After staying up so late to make his carving perfect and to practice his speech, running down the sidewalk now felt great.

Latrice finally caught up with him at the center. She was wearing her Zulu costume with swirls of reds and golds. She held her head erect from the tall, coiled necklace made of wrapped foil.

"That looks tough," Ron said.

"Thanks. But it would look better with that headband. You know, the one in the Sav-a-Lot window."

Ron did not answer. He was watching all the people in African costumes. Some wore robes and turbans. Others wore airy tops with flowing sleeves. Still others were wrapped in rich cloths with glittery threads.

And long tables lined the walls with many baskets of fruits and vegetables.

"Is this a fruit market?" asked Ron.

"No, these displays are to remind us that Kwanzaa is a harvest celebration. It is to celebrate our rich background as African Americans." Latrice pointed to a large flag. "And that is the Kwanzaa flag. It's called the *bendera*."

Ron noticed it had red, black, and green stripes.

"Be right back." Latrice suddenly disappeared into the crowd.

Ron tried to look cool. But the heavy crowd and the throbbing drums made him a little nervous.

Then Ron saw him. By the tall drum stood Big Bad Butler and his buddy. Their upper chests were bare except for heavy gold chains.

Ron looked at Butler's muscles. They made his nose start to throb.

"Here." Latrice swerved back into view from behind a woman with a basket on her head.

"Try this."

"What are they?"

"Honey cakes from Africa." She took a bite. "Mmmmm."

Ron shook his head. "Thanks. But my stomach feels messed with."

He looked around. "Where's the contest?"

Latrice pointed up to a stage. "There. We wait until they call our numbers."

"Then what?"

"Then we walk up there and face the crowd." She handed him a card. "I am Number Four, and you are Number Five. Cool, huh?"

"Crowd?" he asked in a thin voice. "I thought we just stood before a judge."

Latrice nibbled Ron's cake. "No, dum-dum. We perform before a judge and a crowd." She took a deep bow. "That way we get applause."

Ron stepped backward. He did not want a crowd. He did not want applause. He looked at the alligator in his hand. He did not even want this dumb carving!

Throwing down the number, he began to run. Holding on to his cap, he wove in and out of costumed people. Get out, was all he could think about. *Get out . . . get out . . . get out.*

"Ron, wait!"

But Ron ran fast. He ran around men beating tall drums. He ran past women selling herbs and flowers. He ran through tents made of colorful rugs.

Oops! He tripped on a rug roll.

Boom! He sprawled on the floor.

Suddenly he felt strong hands lift him to his feet.

"Up we go, my man," said a man in a gold turban. He wore a name tag that said OFFICIAL. "Say, what's this?"

"My baseball cap."

"No, this." The man in the turban picked up

Ron's alligator. He studied it from all sides. "My, my, what a fine alligator."

"It is?" Ron reached for it.

"Well, it sure looks like an alligator to me."

"No, I mean, is it fine?"

The man laughed. "Why, that dude is so real it could taste your finger." He jumped back and grabbed his hand. "See? It bit me."

Ron laughed.

"There you are!" Latrice shouted. She caught up, breathless. "Why'd you do that? Hurry! The contest is starting."

She nudged Ron through the crowd.

"Thanks, mister," he called over his shoulder.

"Gran is already here," Latrice continued. "She is in the front row. She even borrowed Mrs. Perkins's camera."

Gran is here? thought Ronald. At least Gran won't laugh at me.

6
The Contest

Ron had never seen so many faces. And they were all looking at him. He felt like a million eyes were scraping over his shaky body.

"I'm scared," he whispered to Latrice. "I don't want to do this. I mean it."

"Shhhh. They're starting."

A tall man in a robe stepped up to the microphone. He greeted the audience in several different languages, then he said, "Number One, please."

A girl with cornrows stepped forward. She looked smart to Ron. Real smart. She announced she was going to recite a poem. "It is a poem about freedom." She then recited it in the Swahili language.

Everyone clapped. Even Ron clapped. He liked the sound of the words.

Number Two was a boy with a bare chest and lots of beads and amulets. His hips were wrapped with red cloth.

"I am dressed as a member of the Ewe tribe," he announced. His voice trembled slightly. "This tribe often used drums to send messages." He began to beat two tall drums and explained the message. The audience began to move to the cadence. He then beat an abrupt rhythm, saying this was a warning of war.

Ron didn't know anything about the messages. He just felt his heart pounding to the drumbeat.

"Just one more," Latrice whispered, "then me."

Ron swallowed hard. That meant he was two more away from disaster. He tried to find Gran out there. But his eyes wouldn't focus. He didn't even have to look to his left—he knew too well Big Bad Butler was standing right there. So he just kept staring at his feet.

Number Three turned out to be Butler and his partner. They sprang forward, acting like a stage was no big deal. Striking a semicrouched position, each held a stick in front of his chest. With the other hand, each brandished a long shaft.

"We are of the Pondo tribe," Big Bad Butler announced proudly. "Young men of that tribe learn to protect themselves through warrior games." He wielded the carved stick. "Many treasure their practice weapons." They then began to circle each other slowly. Suddenly Butler made a jab at his opponent.

The audience gasped.

Now the two boys began to slash and swipe at each other furiously. Grunting and shouting, they sparred back and forth across the stage.

Everyone sat forward.

All at once the tall boy made a double thrust, sending Butler's carved cane sliding across the stage.

The tall boy held up his sparring stick in victory.

The crowd cheered.

Ron looked down at his feet again. I hope they don't judge for excitement, he thought.

At last Latrice danced onto the stage. She whirled and swayed. She bent and twisted. Ron felt proud. She is really good, he thought. The audience must have thought so, too. They began to clap to the beat.

"Yea, Latrice!" Ron heard Gran shouting from the front row.

Ron couldn't help it. He waved at Gran.

He was still looking at Gran when he realized the clapping had stopped. His sister had now returned. She was breathless but smiling. "What did you think?"

But Ron didn't have time to answer.

"Number Five, please."

Ron froze. Latrice nudged him toward the mike. He walked forward on rubbery knees.

Ronald looked down at Gran, who was smiling and nodding. Then he looked at his carving.

Then he closed his eyes.

"This is an alligator," he began, and he opened his eyes. "I carved it. It is a sign of freedom to the Baule tribe." He rubbed a sweaty palm across his jeans.

"A legend says that once the enemy had trapped this tribe at a river. The Baule people begged the alligators for help. So the alligators made a bridge by lying side by side." He adjusted the brim of his cap. "Then the African people walked to freedom." He took a deep breath. "Freedom is a wonderful gift," he continued. "So now the alligator is an African sign of freedom."

The crowd cheered and whistled. Gran shouted, "That's my smart grandson!"

Latrice poked him. "That was great. I bet we tie."

Ron did not care. It was over, over, over, and he was still alive.

7
Who Gets the Money?

There were other acts. Ron saw more people going up to the mike. But he couldn't pay attention. His heart was still thudding in his ears.

Suddenly Latrice elbowed him. "Hear that? There's a break, then the judges' decision."

"Good," Ron answered limply. He needed to find a seat somewhere. His knees were still wobbly.

"I'm going down to see Gran." Latrice ran to the edge of the stage and jumped down.

"Me, too!" shouted Ron. Gran give them both a big hug, then a noisy kiss.

In a few minutes the announcer tapped on the mike. "Attention! Attention, everybody!"

The contestants scrambled back onstage.

"There is an interesting dilemma," the announcer informed the crowd. "The judges have declared a tie!"

Latrice squeezed Ron's arm. "What did I tell you?"

"Ouch!" he protested. Her nails were digging deep.

"Get ready!" she whispered excitedly.

"The tie is between . . . "

The audience grew very quiet.

"Number One and Number Five!"

Ron turned to give his winning sister a high five. But she was pushing him forward.

"Yea, Ron!" she called from behind him.

"Hey, wait a—" But he stopped. He was now standing in front of the microphone. And next to him stood Miss Swahili Poem. *She* was Number One—not Latrice.

The announcer said, "The judges felt all displays were great. But they felt the theme of freedom made these two very special." His voice softened. "Freedom is a theme dear to Kwanzaa and all African Americans."

The crowd thundered with applause.

Gran was waving her purse.

Ron looked back to see Latrice waving. She was smiling. But her eyes looked funny.

"Here we are, young man." The announcer handed Ron twenty-five dollars.

Ron stared at the money. It was the most money he had ever had.

But by now the crowd was on the stage. Strangers were patting Ronald on the back. Some even asked to see his carving. But the crowd did not stop Gran. She squeezed both Latrice and Ronald to herself.

"My smart grandbabies," she announced as they left the stage.

Ron quickly tucked the crisp bills in his baseball cap. "Let's go celebrate!" he shouted. "My treat."

"Hey, there, my man!"

Ron turned to see the official with the gold

turban who had helped him to his feet. "That was great, Alligator Man."

Ron laughed. "Thanks to you."

"Not me, friend. Did I not tell you he was fine?" The man patted Ron's alligator. "So what are your plans? Buy your friend there a zoo? Fly him to Africa?"

"No, sir," Ron said. He felt for the bulge of his money under the cap. "I'm going to buy Gran thread of every color."

"You are?" She gave him a big noisy kiss.

"Then a hammer for myself." He almost added "screwdriver," but he looked over at Latrice. "And a headband for my sister," he added.

Latrice looked up. Her eyes grew as round as Gran's cookies. "You're serious?"

Again Ronald nodded.

Latrice suddenly threw her arms around her brother. "Ohhh!"

Ron fought free of her bear hug. "Yes, the one

at—" But he stopped. He looked down at his winning carving. It was broken in three pieces.

"Oh, no!" said Gran as she made clicking sounds. "And you worked so hard on it, too, baby."

"Hey," the man said, "I'm really sorry about that."

"Oh, it's okay, I—" But Ron looked up to see the man wasn't talking to him. He was talking to Big Bad Butler, who was passing by. "That is one fine piece of work." He nodded to the cane.

Butler looked sad. His lower lip even trembled a little. "I know." He looked at the cane now without a handle. The handle was tucked into his sash. "And Mama's gonna get me good. It was her daddy's."

The man shook his head. "That's tough, son. Maybe there's somebody who can—"

"Hey!" Gran interjected. "Let my grandson here have a look. There's nothing he can't fix. Right, Trice?"

"Right!" Latrice agreed.

Butler eyed Ron for a moment, then cautiously handed him both pieces.

Ron couldn't help but run his hand admiringly over the fine workmanship. Then he studied the break.

Despite the noisy crowd, the five grew very quiet. After careful scrutiny, Ron said at last, "You know, once I get my new hammer with its special claw, I can work this stub out. Then I can glue it to the shaft. With a little shaving, it can fit back in the handle good as new."

"That's my Alligator Man," said the official proudly, slapping Ron's shoulder.

Butler's eyes grew wide. "You're not foolin'? You really think so?"

"Don't see why not." Ron told him to come over to Gran's that afternoon.

Suddenly Latrice grabbed Ron's hand. "Oh, don't worry, Butler," she called. "My smart brother can do anything. Right, Gran?"

"Right! Why, there's no end to my Little Man's talent."

Ron cringed.

But Butler didn't seem to pay any attention. "Could I come over now maybe? Or meet you there?"

"Sorry." Ron smiled at Gran. "Gran, my sister, and I have some celebrating to do. But I'll be home around three o'clock with my new hammer."

"Cool!" shouted Big Bad Butler as a smile spread across his face.

Just as Ron and his family hurried off to enjoy their Kwanzaa day, Butler called Ron's name.

"Yeah?" Ron asked, turning.

"Thanks." Big Bad Butler called in a small voice. "I mean it."

Ron didn't say anything. He just thought smiley thoughts as he joined Latrice and Gran. This was one Kwanzaa celebration he would *never* forget!